FEAST FOR 10

CATHRYN FALWELL

CLARION BOOKS, NEW YORK

HOUGHTON MIFFLIN COMPANY

BOSTON

ATLANTA   DALLAS   GENEVA, ILLINOIS   PALO ALTO   PRINCETON

Feast for 10, by Cathryn Falwell. Copyright © 1993 by Cathryn Falwell. Reprinted by permission of Clarion Books, a division of Houghton Mifflin Company. All rights reserved.

2000 Impression
Houghton Mifflin Edition, 1997

No part of this work may be reproduced or transmitted in any form or by any means, electronic or mechanical, including photocopying and recording, or by any information storage or retrieval system, without the prior written permission of the copyright owner unless such copying is expressly permitted by federal copyright law. With the exception of nonprofit transcription in Braille, Houghton Mifflin is not authorized to grant permission for further uses of this work. Permission must be obtained from the individual copyright owner as identified herein.

Printed in the U.S.A.

ISBN: 0-395-81084-1

6789-B-02 01 00

For
my family

in
loving memory
of
my grandmothers

Willie Mae McMullen Chauvin
and
Evelyn Haning Falwell

who often made
feasts for plenty

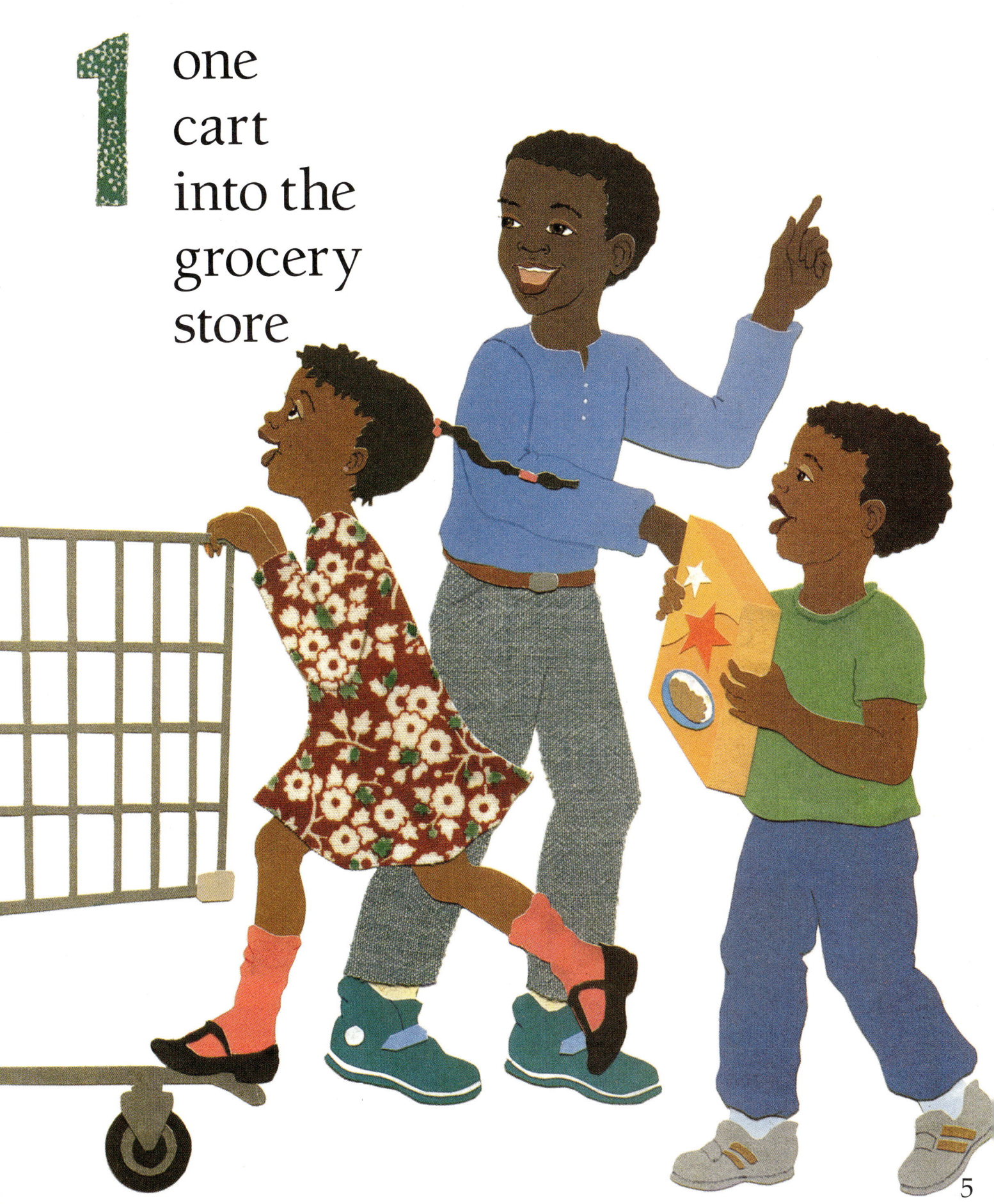

2 two pumpkins for pie

3 three chickens to fry

4

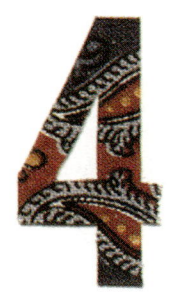

four
children
off to
look for
more

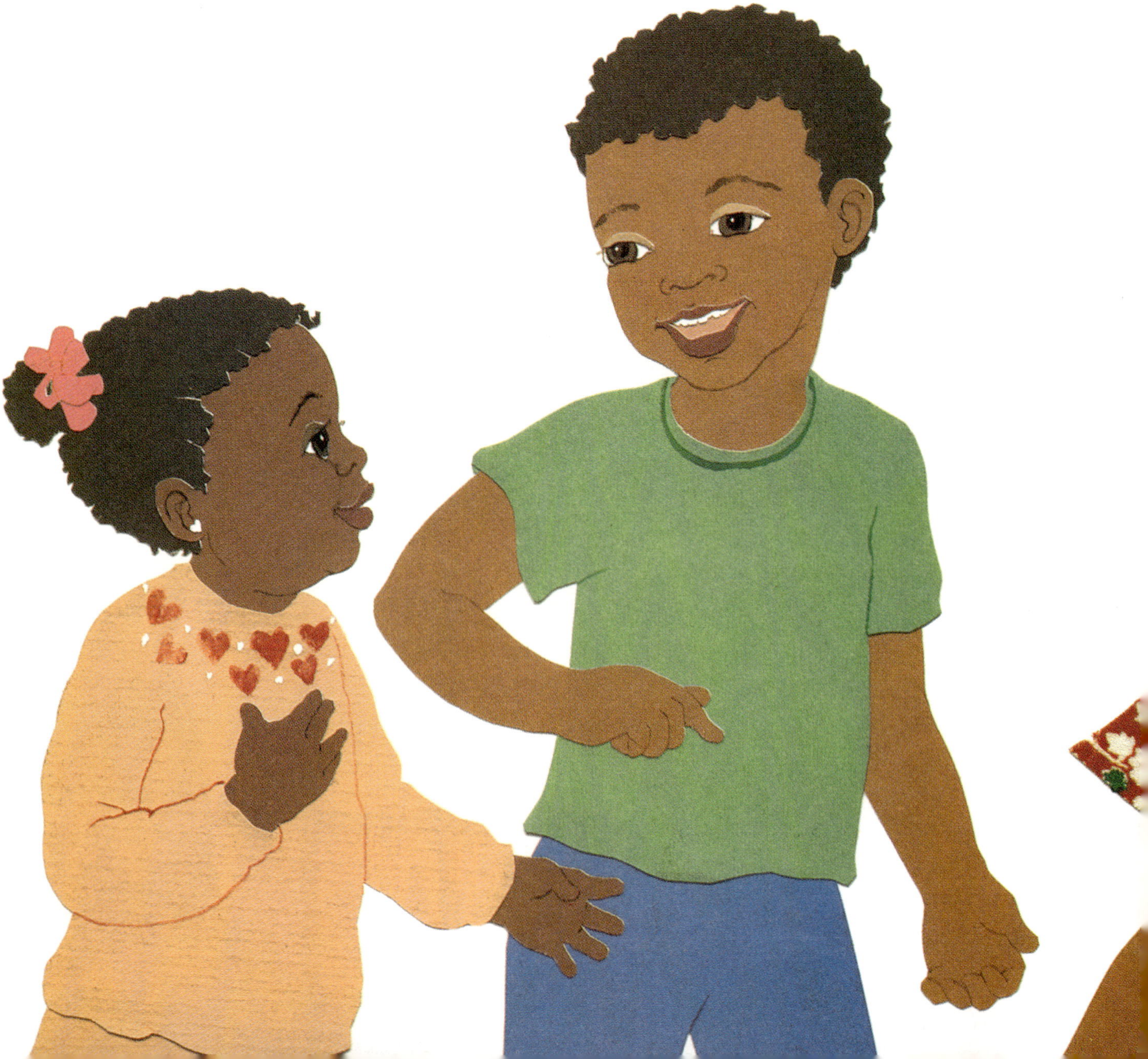

5 five kinds of beans

6 six bunches of greens

7 seven
dill pickles
stuffed in
a jar

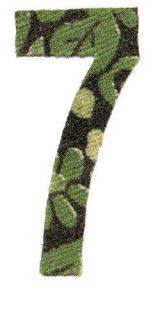

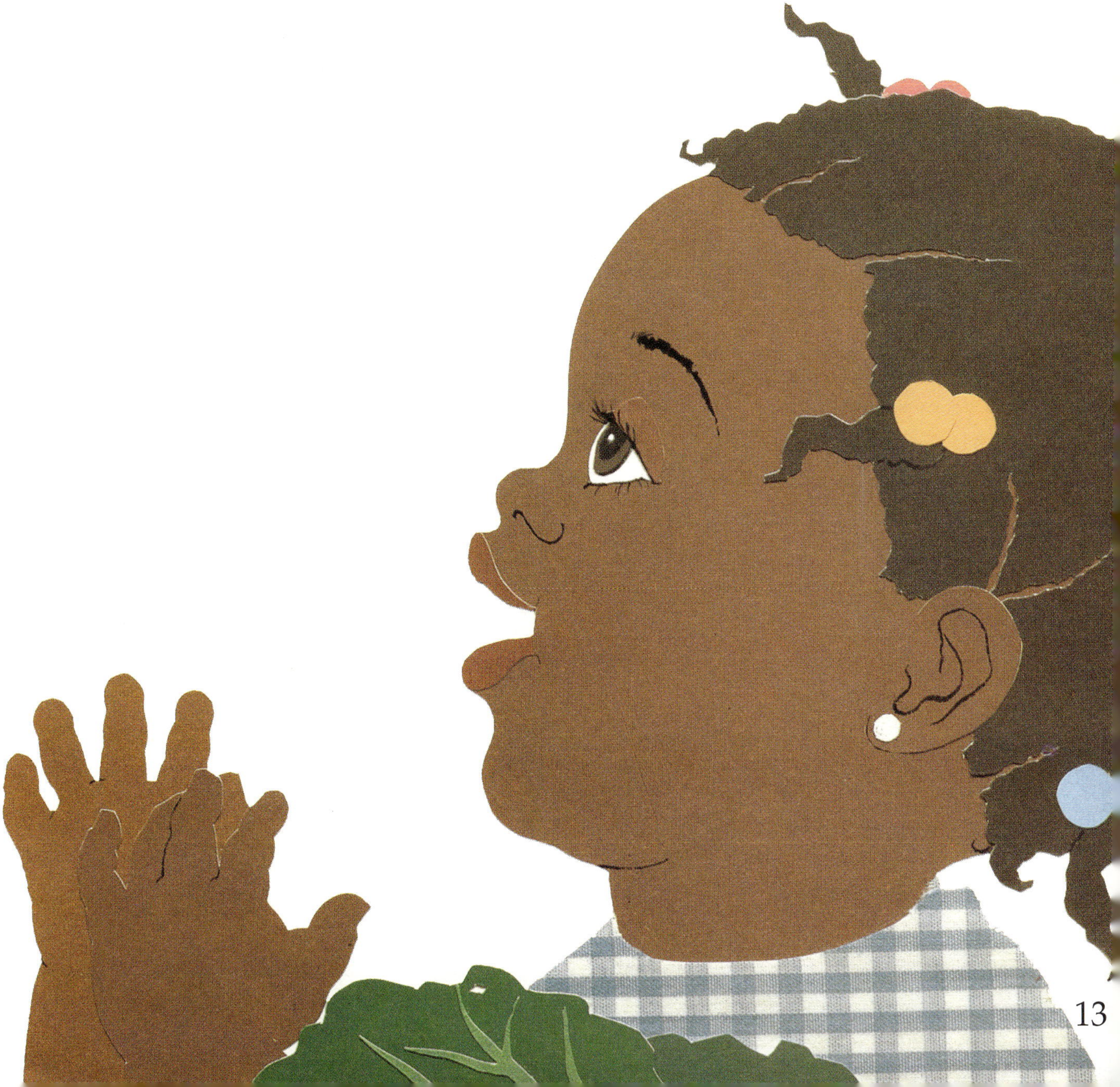

 eight
ripe
tomatoes

9 nine plump potatoes

Then . . .

1 one car home from the grocery store

2 two will look

3 three will cook

4 four will taste and ask for more

6 six pots and pans

7 seven more carrots to wash and peel

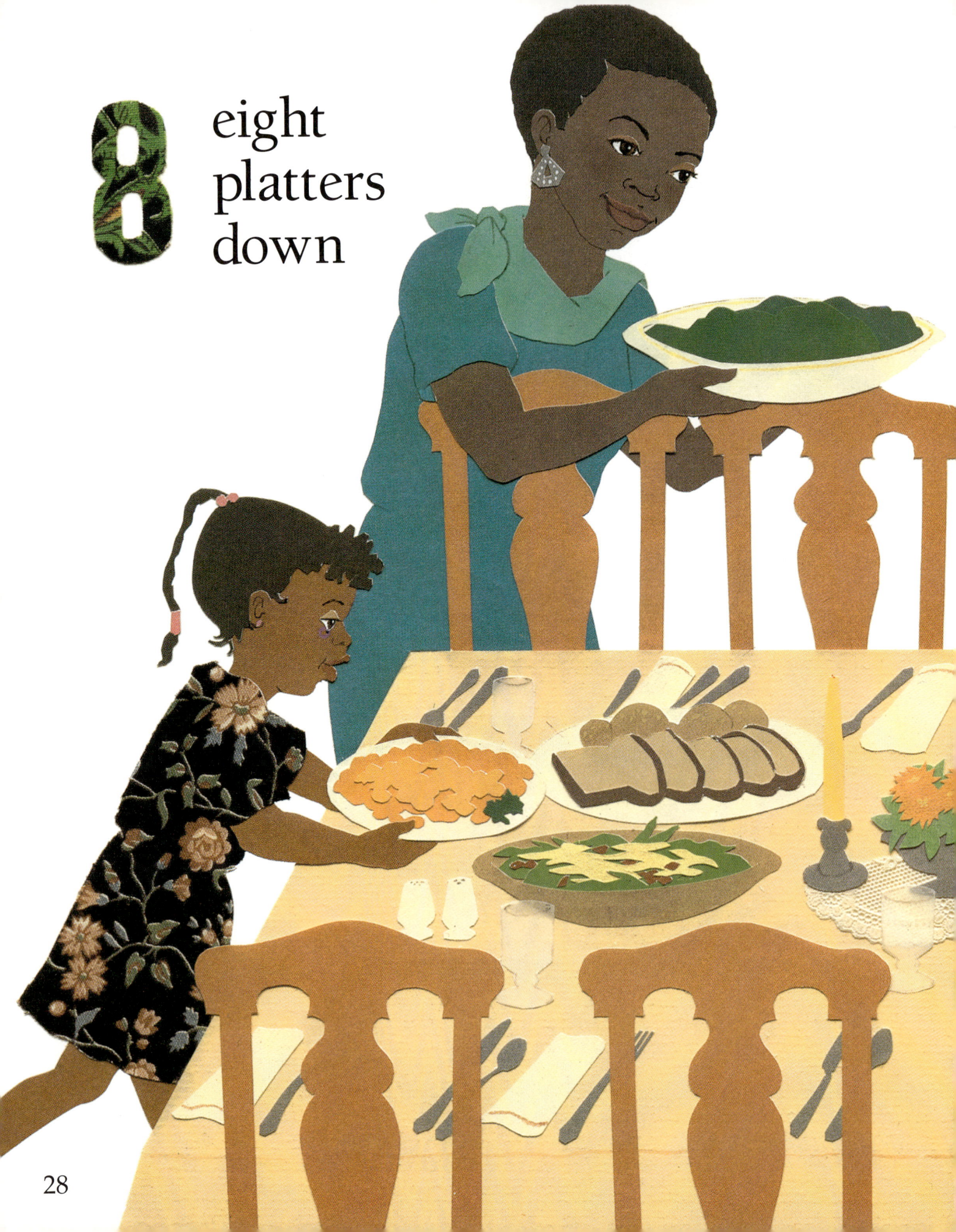

8 eight platters down

10 ten hungry folks to share the meal!